About this book

Many children have difficulty puzzling out letters because they
are abstract symbols. Letterland's worldwide success is all about its
enduring characters who give these symbols life and stop them from
being abstract. In this book we meet Uppy Umbrella and Vase of Violets.
Their story is carefully designed to emphasise the sounds that the letters
'U' and 'V' make in words. This definitive, original story book is an instant
collector's classic, making learning fun for a new generation of readers.

A TEMPLAR BOOK

This edition published in the UK in 2008 by Templar Publishing
an imprint of The Templar Company plc,
The Granary, North Street, Dorking, Surrey, RH4 1DN, UK
www.templarco.co.uk

First published by Thomas Nelson & Sons Ltd, 1993
Devised and produced by The Templar Company plc

1 3 5 7 9 8 6 4 2

ISBN 978-1-84011-772-1

Printed in China

Classic LETTERLAND *Storybooks*

Uppy Umbrella in Volcano Valley

Also featuring **V**ase of **V**iolets

Written by Stephanie Laslett

Illustrated by
Maggie Downer

templar publishing

Uppy Umbrella looked out of her kitchen window and smiled happily. The sun shone brightly and a butterfly fluttered by on the warm breeze.

"A perfect washday!" she thought.

Soon Uppy was up to her elbows in soapy suds as she rubbed and scrubbed her clothes in the washtub.

"Hum, ti tum, ti tum, and
rub, ti tub, ti tub," she hummed,
as bubbles floated up around her.

But in the garden, the gentle breeze had turned into a blustery wind!

"Oh, *do* stay still!" Uppy grumbled as she struggled to peg her washing on the clothes line.

Suddenly a strong gust of wind pushed Uppy Umbrella right into the air.

"Put me down!" cried Uppy, but the wind wouldn't listen. With a "whoosh!" it blew her right out of the garden.

Up, up she went until she found herself blowing right over the Letterland castle.

Poor Uppy Umbrella!
One minute she was right side up.
The next minute she was upside
down. The wind was having lots of fun
– but Uppy was not enjoying herself.
She was very upset.

Now, far below her she could see the
docks. There was Mr O busy on the
docks with Oscar Orange, and Lucy by
her lighthouse.

"Help, help!" called Uppy. "I'm
blowing away!" but no-one could
hear her. Her voice was lost on the
blustery wind.

Soon the castle and docks were far behind her. Uppy was swept high above a deep valley full of violets. A thick carpet of beautiful flowers stretched as far as the eye could see!

The wind swept her on. Now the sides of the valley were steeper. A vivid flash of light lit up the sky. A thundering rumble filled the air.

"Flashes and rumbles!" cried Uppy. "It's the old volcano spitting again."

The wind swept her closer and closer until Uppy landed – thump, bump, bump – right on the side of the volcano.

Uppy tried to jump up. But the end of her umbrella was stuck in a small tunnel.

"Just my luck!" muttered Uppy. Then she heard a muffled voice mumbling below her.

"What a hubbub and a hullabaloo!" it fussed. The voice was coming from the tunnel. Uppy could feel something pushing her. With each push the small voice grunted, "Uh, uh, uh!"

But the pushing and grunting did no good. Uppy was still stuck fast.

Next Uppy heard a scrabbling noise. All of a sudden an unhappy little face poked out of the ground. It was a vole – and he was very upset!

"Look at all this dust and mud! You've messed up my home!" he grumbled.

"I am very sorry," said Uppy Umbrella. "The blustery wind just blew me here and I couldn't stop."

"Well, you'll have to go," said the vole. "You're blocking my tunnel." He took hold of Uppy's handle and tugged with all his might. But it was no good. She was still stuck tight.

Uppy was uncomfortable and unhappy. Would she be stuck here forever?

She thought of home and her washing on the line. She remembered her journey high above Letterland. Then she remembered how she was swept over the Valley of Violets.

"Of course!" she cried. "Vase of Violets lives near here. She'll know what to do."

The little vole volunteered to find her. Then he scampered off down the side of the volcano.

Soon the vole reached the Valley of Violets. He scurried in and out and over and under the smiling flowers. In very soft voices, the violets whispered the way to Vase of Violets' home. Their velvet petals stroked his fur as he hurried along.

At last he reached the place where the violets grew thickest of all. There, in the middle of a large circle of flowers, stood Vase of Violets, nodding gently.

"Welcome, little vole," she murmured. "My violets told me you were coming. How can I help you?"

Quickly, the vole explained his problem. "How very vexing for you both," said Vase of Violets. "But I have an idea."

Vase of Violets turned her face to the sky and with a voice like violin music she called, "Vernon Vulture! Are you there?"

Everyone gazed upwards. A large black shadow swept overhead. With wings flapping, a huge vulture landed beside them. The little vole shivered nervously.

"Don't be nervous," laughed Vase of Violets. "Vernon wouldn't hurt a fly." The vulture swivelled his head to face the vole – and winked.

Quickly, Vase of Violets explained her plan. Vernon Vulture gently gripped her vase in his huge claws, the vole scrambled onto his back and together they flew off up the valley.

Back on the volcano Uppy Umbrella was still very upset. Suddenly she saw a small speck high in the sky. Soon the vulture, the vole and the vase were hovering right above her.

"Tip me up," ordered Vase of Violets. "Pour water from my vase. It will loosen the earth around Uppy's umbrella. Then she will come unstuck."

The plan worked beautifully. Uppy laughed as she struggled up out of the mud.

"What an unusual rescue! Thank you very, very much!"

The wind had died down now
and the volcano was quiet, too.
Uppy remembered her washing.
Her clothes would be nice and
dry by now.

"I must be on my way, everybody,"
she said.

"Would you like a lift?" asked
Vernon, hopefully. "Vulture Voyages
at your service."

"No, thanks," laughed Uppy, as she
waved goodbye. "I think I can trust
the wind to behave this time!"

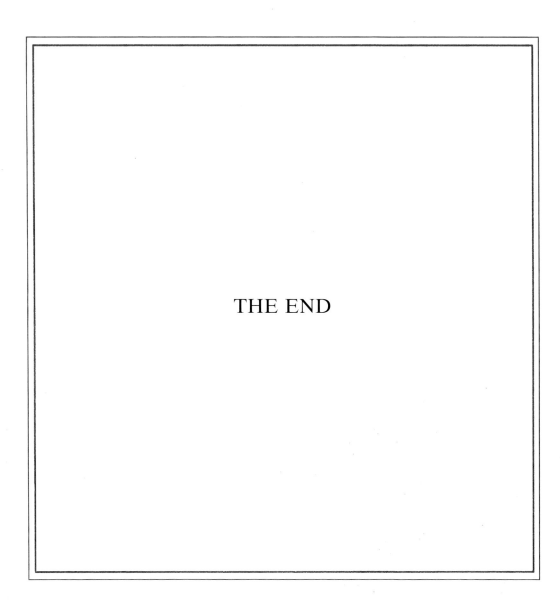

THE END